This book belongs to

....

....

GW Publishing

www.gwpublishing.com

Hamish

This is Hamish the haggis
of the McHaggis clan,
rarely seen by
the eyes of man.

Rupert Harold the Third
is an English gent,
travelling far from
his home in Kent.

Rupert

Our Jeannie's an osprey with wide sweeping wings,
who is easily distracted by all sorts of things.

Jeannie

Angus

Young Angus is cheeky and likes playing the fool,
whatever he's doing, he's got to look cool.

For Stuart
for always being there. L.S.

For Pete
with love and thanks. S.J.C.

Text and Illustrations copyright © Linda Strachan and Sally J. Collins

www.lindastrachan.com
www.hamishmchaggis.co.uk

First Published in paperback in Great Britain 2005
Reprinted 2007, 2009, 2011 and 2013

Design - Veneta Altham

Reprographics - GWP Graphics

Printed in China

Published by

GW Publishing
PO Box 15070
Dunblane
FK15 5AN
Scotland

www.gwpublishing.com

ISBN 09546701-5-9
978-0-9546701-5-3

Hamish McHaggis

and the search for
The Loch Ness Monster

By Linda Strachan
Illustrated by Sally J. Collins

In a secret glen in the Highlands of Scotland, snuggled underneath the mountains, there's a little place called Coorie Doon. Here you will find the McHaggis Hoggle, the home of Hamish McHaggis and his friends.

Snug in his cosy Hoggle, Hamish McHaggis was settling down to munch on his favourite snack, roasted heather nuts and wild mint.

Rupert waved a leaflet in front of Hamish. "This is rubbish! Everyone knows there's no such thing as the Loch Ness Monster."

"Nonsense, of course she's real," spluttered Hamish. "Nessie's a good friend of Jeannie's."

Angus giggled. "Just wait until Jeannie hears that you think Nessie's not real. She'll flip!"

Jeannie crash-landed through the doorway, fanning out her wings in a cloud of dust.

"Orgsh! Pleagh!" Hamish spluttered. "Jeannie!"
"Oops, sorry. I was thinking about something else,"
Jeannie apologised as she skidded to a stop.

"Jeannie is a clumsy clops," Angus chuckled in a sing-song voice, wiping the dust out of his eyes. "Guess what, Jeannie? Rupert doesn't believe in Nessie. I think we should take him to meet her."

"Why, yes," agreed Jeannie. "What a good idea."

"Yippee! We're going to Loch Ness," Angus squealed.

Everyone started preparing for the trip.

"Let me see, I promised Nessie I would bring her some golf clubs next time I visited her, and I think I should take my rain hat, just in case the weather turns wet."

"Mmmh, what should I put in the picnic basket? Sandwiches, yes, and some apples and perhaps a few nuts. Oh, and I must remember to take my new scarf."

"Mustn't forget the camera,
and my briefcase with the maps
and my binoculars, and of
course my mobile phone."

"Skateboard, CD player
and headphones-
they'll all fit in my
backpack."

Once everything was packed into the Whirry-Bang they were ready to set off.

"Hurry up everyone." Hamish shouted as he tooted on the horn and checked his picnic box for the fourth time, just in case he had forgotten anything. "Angus! We're leaving!"

Toot!

Angus skidded down the nearest tree
and leapt into the Whirry-Bang. "I'm here!"
He tossed his backpack into the back.

So with a

Whirrrr

and a

clunk

a Squee

and a loud

Bang

they set off for Loch Ness.

"Are we there yet?" Angus moaned from the back.

"We've just left," said Hamish. "Hold on, everyone!"

The Whirry-Bang flew round a corner on two wheels. Jeannie flapped her wings and took off, deciding it would be safer to fly.

"Are we there, yet?" Angus moaned again, a few minutes later.

"We've got to go to Inverness first." Rupert showed Angus the map.

"I know that!" said Angus. "But are we there yet?"

"Och, haud yer wheesht!" muttered Hamish. Rupert looked puzzled.

"It just means 'be quiet'," Hamish explained.

When they reached Loch Ness the road was busy with cars and buses taking tourists to look for Nessie. "She won't come out just now," Hamish told Rupert. "Nessie always hides from the tourists. She's very shy."

"I'll go and see if I can find her," Jeannie
said, and she flew off across the loch.

"I'm hungry. Let's go and find a place for our
picnic," piped up Angus.

"I'm hungry, too," agreed Hamish.

"You're always hungry! I wanted to look for the
Monster," Rupert grumbled as he packed up his
binoculars and climbed back into the Whirry-Bang.

"Get out of the way, Angus!"

splash!

Jeannie put one foot out, trying to slow herself down. A fountain of water splashed everyone but Angus ducked down and Jeannie missed him by a feather.

"Did you find Nessie?" Hamish asked, squeezing water out of his soggy sandwich.

"No, no one's seen her today, but the seagulls said she might be at Drumnadrochit, near the Visitor Centre." Jeannie shook the water from her wings and showered everyone again.
"I think we should look there next."
So they finished their picnic quickly and set off again in the Whirry-Bang.

They found lots of Nessie toys at the Visitors Centre.

"So what does Nessie look like?" asked Rupert. "A bit like this fluffy one?"

"Perhaps more like this one."

"Nessie's not really like any of these," Jeannie said. "She's probably gone home to her cave for some peace and quiet, away from the tourists.

I think we should go and have a look in her cave. It's not far."

Hamish led the way into Nessie's cave. He lit a candle but when the flame fluttered in the breeze it made scary shapes on the walls.

Angus was hiding behind Rupert. "It's dark and scary in here. Do you think Nessie will mind us coming to visit her?"

"Don't worry, Angus," Jeannie said. "Nessie loves having visitors."

They went deeper and deeper into the dark cave. The wind howled and the candle flickered. Angus was scared.

"I can see a light over there." Hamish whispered, trying very hard to be brave.

The cave opened out into Nessie's
bright and cosy living room. "She's not
here!" said Angus. "Look, she's left a note."

The note said;

Dear Milkman
No milk for the next two
weeks please. I'm away
on my holidays.
                    Nessie

So they packed up and set
off in the Whirry-Bang on their
way back to Coorie Doon.

"I knew we wouldn't find
Nessie," mumbled Rupert.

When they got home there was a
postcard from Nessie lying on the doormat.

DID YOU KNOW?

Coorie Doon means to nestle or cosy down comfortably.

Haud yer wheesht! means be quiet!

Blether means to gossip or chatter.

Droothy means thirsty.

Shoogly means shaky.

Brae means hill.

Glen means valley.

Angus is a Pine Marten.

Ospreys usually live near water.

Pine Martens are expert at climbing trees.

It is commonly thought that a **Haggis** has three legs, two long and one short. This always makes Hamish laugh.

Hedgehogs and **Pine Martens** are not usually the best of friends.

Loch Ness is 23 miles long and a mile wide.

Drumnadrochit is a village at the side of Loch Ness.

**Hamish McHaggis
and The search for The
Loch Ness Monster**

978-0-9546701-5-3

**Hamish McHaggis
and The Edinburgh Adventure**

978-0-9546701-7-7

**Hamish McHaggis
and The Ghost of Glamis**

978-0-9546701-9-1

**Hamish McHaggis
and The Skye Surprise**

978-0-9546701-8-4

**Hamish McHaggis
and The Skirmish at Stirling**

978-0-9551564-1-0

**Hamish McHaggis
and The Wonderful Water Wheel**

978-0-9551564-0-3

**Hamish McHaggis
and The Wonderful Water Wheel**

978-0-9554145-5-8

**Hamish McHaggis
and The Clan Gathering**

978-0-9561211-2-7

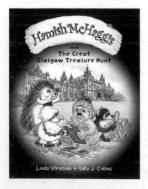

**Hamish McHaggis
and The Great
Glasgow Treasure Hunt**

978-0-9570844-0-7

**Hamish McHaggis
Activity and Story Book**

978-0-9554145-1-0

Also by the
same author
and illustrator

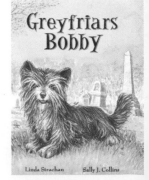

Greyfriars Bobby

978-0-9551564-2-7